Th
Midnight Feast

Hannah Cole

Illustrated by
Kate Aldous

Julia MacRae Books
A division of Walker Books

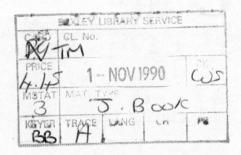
Text © 1990 Hannah Cole
Illustrations © 1990 Kate Aldous
First published in Great Britain 1990
by Julia MacRae Books
A division of Walker Books Ltd
87 Vauxhall Walk
London SE11 5HJ

British Library Cataloguing in Publication Data
Cole, Hannah
The midnight feast
I. Title   II. Series
823'.914[J]

ISBN 0-86203-449-3

Typeset by Action Typesetting Limited Gloucester
Reproduced, printed and bound in Great Britain by
BPCC Hazell Books
Aylesbury, Bucks, England
Member of BPCC Ltd.

Contents

Also by Hannah Cole

1 The new friend

One day Rose forgot where the front door key was. Mum hid it in a different place each week, somewhere in the back yard. She didn't trust Rose to take the key to school with her in case she lost it. Rose was supposed to come straight home from school, get the key from its hiding place, and go indoors to wait until her sister Liz came home from the big school on her bicycle. Then Liz was in charge until Mum came home from work.

It was Monday, the first day of a new hiding place. Rose looked in all the places they had used before. The key was not behind the dustbin, or in the crack in the fence, or on the window-sill. Of course Liz would remember where they had agreed to hide it, but Rose wanted to be indoors before Liz came home. Liz would say that she was too young to come home on her own, and perhaps Rose would have to go in next door after school and play with Tanya. Sometimes she liked Tanya, but she didn't always want to go round there, especially when the baby was crying and Tanya's mother was shouting.

Rose looked round for good hiding places. She lifted a few rocks, although she knew that the key wasn't under them. The little yard looked so empty.

On the other side of the fence, sheets were hanging on the washing line in Tanya's yard. They were pink sheets with rainbows at the ends, and Rose knew they were off Tanya's bed. She wondered if Tanya had wet the bed last night. One thing Rose didn't like about Tanya's mother was that she shouted at Tanya for wetting the bed, even though Tanya didn't do it on purpose.

Rose tried to remember what Mum had said that morning as they all left the house. Mum had told Rose to wear her coat at playtime because it was cold. Rose had told Mum that she should

have taken her swimming money to school last
week, and Mum had said that she would find it
tonight. Rose remembered walking to the corner
with Mum and saying goodbye, but she couldn't
remember anything about the key.

Rose thought of going to the bank where Mum
worked. Even if Mum was not at the counter,
Rose could wave to her through the glass, and
Mum could come and tell her where the key was.
Mum wouldn't be pleased, because at work she
was meant to concentrate on bank business, and
not spend time thinking about her children or
their lost keys.

"Want to come and play?" Tanya shouted
through the fence. Rose could only see the top of

her head with its ribbon. That was an annoying
thing about Tanya. She always wore ribbons in
her hair. Rose went to the broken place and
looked through.

"Did you see my mum hiding the key this
morning?" she asked. "I can't remember where
she said she put it."

"I was having a bath this morning," said
Tanya. "I was nearly late for school."

"Did you wet the bed?" said Rose.

"No, it wasn't me," said Tanya. "It was the
baby. Mum let her sleep in my bed last night and
her nappy came undone and we woke up all
sopping wet."

"I wouldn't want a leaky baby like that in my
bed," said Rose.

"She's nice and cuddly," said Tanya. "Do you
want to come in and see her have her tea? She
can hold her own spoon now. It doesn't always go
in her mouth, though. She put some food in her
eye this morning."

"I might come and watch one day," said Rose.
"But I'm supposed to stay indoors until Mum
comes home. I can't today, because I don't know

where the key is. By the way, I've got a new friend now, so I may not be playing with you quite so often."

She went round to the front of the house again, and wondered whether to set off to the bank. Far down the road she saw Liz on her bicycle.

"What are you doing out here?" Liz asked. "You're supposed to go straight in and shut the door."

"I was playing hopscotch in the yard," said Rose. "I thought I heard you coming."

"Is the back door open?" said Liz.

"No," said Rose. "I haven't been indoors yet. The key's still in the hiding place."

"Well, go and get it, then," said Liz.

"Can you get it while you're putting your bike away?" said Rose. "I need the loo. I can't move." She crossed her legs over each other.

"Baby," said Liz. She wheeled her bicycle round to the yard and came back with her school bag and the key.

"Quick," said Rose.

Liz opened the door, and Rose ran indoors and straight upstairs to the bathroom. She wondered

where the key had been hidden, and reminded
herself that she must find out for tomorrow.

Down in the kitchen, Liz had put the kettle on.
Rose was sure that Liz didn't really like tea,
because she always drank it in tiny sips and made
a funny face. Rose thought that Liz only made
herself tea because it was something that she was
allowed to do and Rose was not. Mum said that
Rose wasn't old enough to use a kettle.

Rose poured herself some milk. She didn't like
milk very much, but Liz hated milk. She said it
made her feel sick to see Rose drinking it,
especially when it made a white moustache on

Rose's lip. So Rose made sure that the milk slopped up a little way over her lip, and she made delicious drinking noises to remind Liz how creamy the milk was.

"Little pig," said Liz.

"You're a big pig," said Rose.

"Mum said we're not to argue while she is out," said Liz.

"You started," said Rose.

"I did not," said Liz. "I was just trying to improve your behaviour. I'm going to do my homework now, so you'd better be quiet."

"I didn't want to talk to you anyway," said Rose.

It wasn't really true. She had meant to tell Liz about her new best friend. Now she would have to wait until Mum came home. She rinsed out her milk cup and went and found her recorder.

"Oh, not that row," said Liz. "I'm trying to concentrate."

"Mrs Prout said I must practise my high E," said Rose. She played her high E lots of times.

"Can't you play something quiet?" said Liz.

"Shall I play with my Lego?" said Rose.

"Yes, please," said Liz. "I need to think."

So Rose got out the biscuit tin where they kept
the Lego, and shook it a little so that the
interesting bits would come to the top. Liz sighed
and folded her mouth up into an elder-sister
shape, but she said nothing, so Rose settled down
to make a transforming space buggy.

2 No feast

When Mum's key rattled in the lock, Rose ran out into the hall.

"Mum, I've got a new friend!"

"That's nice. Who is it? Ooh, I could do with a cup of tea."

"It's Shireen. I've moved to sit next to her, and we were partners in P.E., and she's lent me her best pen, and, Mum, can she come home after school one day this week?"

Mum went into the kitchen and looked in the oven. Liz had already turned it on, and there was a nice smell from the casserole and baked potatoes which Mum had got ready in the morning. Mum put the kettle on.

"Shall I get your tea ready?" said Rose. "You like this cup best, don't you, Mum? Or do you want the spotty one? I've got a tea-bag ready. Can I put the sugar in? Can I ask her to tea, Mum? Tomorrow?"

"Set the table for me, love, while I go and get changed, and then you can tell me all about her."

Rose listened to the kettle as the water inside began to get excited. She hopped from foot to foot, impatient to tell Mum all about Shireen.

At last Mum came downstairs in her ordinary old clothes.

"Set the table, I said," said Mum. "Spoons as well for the gravy, and marge for the potatoes."

The kettle hissed and roared and clicked off. Mum poured the boiling water into her cup, and sat down at the table.

Rose took the margarine out of the fridge. She fetched the salt and even thought of a mat for the hot casserole.

"Now," she said. "Can she?"

"Who?" said Mum. "What?"

"Shireen. Can she come to tea?"

"Maybe one day," said Mum. "When I've got a

day off work."

"You never have days off work," said Rose. "I might have to wait for months. She wants to come this week."

"Oh, Rose, you know she can't," said Mum. "We can't invite children round when I'm not even here."

"We would be all right," said Rose. "I never get into any trouble, do I? And it's only for a little while, until Liz comes home. Then she can look after us."

"Look after who?" said Liz. She had come into the kitchen and was neatening the knives and forks which Rose had laid out.

"Rose wants to ask a friend round," said Mum. "But it's no good."

"I'm not looking after two little kids," said Liz. "And Rose is not fit to be left on her own. She was playing out in the street when I came home today."

"Rose, you weren't!" said Mum. "You know you're to come straight indoors and stay here."

"I wasn't playing out in the street," said Rose. "I was just looking out for Liz."

"Anyway," said Mum, "I don't suppose Shireen's parents would want her going home to an empty house. Ask her over on Saturday instead. That would be nice."

"Saturday's no good," said Rose. "People are always busy on Saturdays. They go shopping, and

get taken to parks and things. You don't care if I have friends or not. Everyone else has friends home to play after school. And that Amy will invite Shireen if I don't, and then she'll be Amy's best friend instead of mine."

Mum drank her tea and frowned.

"And I promised her we could have beefburgers for tea, because she's allergic to everything else."

"You shouldn't make promises you can't keep," said Liz. "Tell her, Mum."

"What about," said Mum, "what about if she came round for the evening after I get back from work, and stayed the night?"

"Yes!" shouted Rose. "She can come round tonight! I'll ring her! Where's the phone book?"

"Mum!" said Liz. "Did you have to suggest that? Really!"

"Not tonight," said Mum. "It will have to be Friday night. Then it doesn't matter if you stay up late, because there's no school in the morning. You can explain that I don't get home until half-past five."

"We wouldn't stay up late," said Rose. "I promise. Can't it be tomorrow?"

"No, it can't," said Mum. "Where can we put her to sleep, I wonder?"

"She can sleep in my bed," said Rose. "I can sleep on the floor next to her, in a sleeping bag."

"We haven't got a sleeping bag," said Mum.

"No, you two can sleep in my bed. It's big enough for both of you. And I'll sleep in your bed. That will be fine."

"Can we have chocolate fingers for tea?" asked Rose. "Because that's the sort of food she's used to. And she doesn't eat toast for breakfast. She has cereal. It has to be Chokky Pops. She's allergic to the other sorts."

"Don't worry," said Mum. "We won't let her starve."

"Chokky Pops?" said Rose. "Just for a treat, Mum?"

"All right, Chokky Pops. We'll go shopping on Thursday night and get everything we need."

"Lemonade?"

"All right."

"And we can have a midnight feast," said Rose. "What shall we have for our midnight feast?"

"No midnight feasts," said Mum. "I don't want crumbs in my bed, and I don't want to be woken up in the middle of the night, and I don't want you and your friend to be like limp dish-rags in the morning because you've had no sleep. Definitely no midnight feasts."

"I think these potatoes are done," said Liz, looking grown-up with the oven gloves. "Shall I get them out?"

"Shireen is a bit cleaner than us, Mum," said Rose. "I think we'd better dust everything before she comes."

"For goodness' sake," said Mum. "I'm not spring cleaning the house for Shireen."

"Well, I might dust it a bit," said Rose. "Have we got any dusters? And she will need clean sheets on the bed, won't she? Can we iron them so that they have nice straight creases down the middle?"

"They don't need ironing," said Mum. "They are not made of that sort of stuff."

"I think I'd better iron them anyway," said Rose. "I don't want Shireen to think that we are the sort of people who don't iron their sheets."

"Let's have tea," said Mum. "Maybe Shireen won't be allowed to come and stay the night. Maybe she won't even want to."

3 Plans

But Shireen was allowed to come and stay the night. And she wanted to very much. She was looking forward to the lemonade and chocolate fingers, and the Chokky Pops for breakfast. She was looking forward to sleeping in the big bed with Rose. They planned to bounce on it very quietly, and have a careful pillow fight, so as not to mess up Mum's room. She was looking forward to having a shower, because at home they only had a bath. And most of all she was looking forward to the midnight feast.

"It has to be really secret," said Rose. "Because Mum said that a feast was the one thing we were definitely not allowed. We will have to make sure there are no crumbs or she'll notice them."

"It's better if it's secret," said Shireen.

"I've still got some sweets left over from Saturday," said Rose. "I'll save them. And if Mum gives me a chocolate biscuit after swimming, I'll save that too. What else can we have?"

"I'll bring something from home," said Shireen. "My dad goes shopping on Friday, so there's always lots of nice food in the cupboard when I get in. Do you like apple and blackberry pies?"

"I think so," said Rose.

"He usually buys a packet of those."

They planned the feast all week. When Shireen brought a banana to school, Rose put it in her satchel and took it home to hide in her drawer.

"I could have brought an apple," Shireen said, "but apples are noisier when you bite them. It might wake your mother up. Nobody could hear you eating a banana."

"It's Liz that we have to worry about," said Rose. "She's so suspicious. If she thinks that we have a secret, she'll be watching all the time to find out what it is and spoil it."

Shireen didn't have any brothers or sisters.

"Does Liz boss you around?" she asked. "Does she bully you?"

"All the time," said Rose. "Once she twisted my arm on purpose."

Shireen looked nervous.

"It's all right," said Rose. "I won't let her touch you. And I don't see how she can find out about the midnight feast. I only put things in the drawer when she was out of the room, and she's sure to be fast asleep long before midnight. She's always saying that she needs her sleep. She gets angry if I get up early in the morning, because she says it wakes her up."

"Suppose we fall asleep before midnight too?" asked Shireen. "I usually go to sleep at eight o'clock."

Rose hadn't thought of that. She knew that she often fell asleep as soon as she went to bed, even when she planned to stay awake.

"We won't lie down," she said. "We'll sit up and tell each other ghost stories, and it'll be so scary that we won't dare fall asleep. We'll have to talk in whispers, because Mum is sure to tell us to go to sleep if she hears us."

"They mustn't be very scary ghost stories," said Shireen. "Not about people with no heads. I like scary stories, but they give me nightmares, so the doctor said I mustn't listen to that sort of story."

"All right," said Rose. "No people without heads. Just whole ghosts gliding about in the shadows."

"And not too many funny noises."

"They have to make a bit of a noise," said Rose. "Like whooooooo! and aaaaah! But only quietly, because of Mum not hearing."

Shireen didn't mention it to Rose, but she'd never stayed at a friend's house before. Of course, she had stayed at her nan's, but that was different. She was used to staying at her nan's since she was a baby. She hadn't even seen Rose's house before, or met her mother, or the terrible big sister, Liz.

"I would rather have gone just for tea," she said to her mother on Friday morning.

"Rubbish," said her mother. "You'll have a lovely time. And anyway, Rose's mother explained on the phone that you can't go round until she

gets in from work, and it would hardly be worth going unless you stop for the night. She sounded a nice woman. I wouldn't let you go unless I was sure she would take good care of you. And there's always the phone. You can ring me up and I'll come straight round and fetch you home, if you feel homesick. I'll put Poodle in your bag. She'll be company for you in bed."

"Oh no," said Shireen. "I'm not taking Poodle. I'm not a baby."

"We could just pack her, down at the bottom of the bag," her mother suggested. "Then you could get her out if you needed her."

"Of course I won't need her," said Shireen, wondering whether she would be able to sleep without Poodle. Then she remembered the midnight feast. "I'll be fine."

All day at school, Shireen and Rose made plans. They planned which games they were going to play. Rose was going to teach Shireen how to play Flat Fish, and Shireen was going to show Rose how to make a hopping frog out of folded paper. They talked about what they would eat for tea and breakfast. They planned to make a sign for Rose's mum's bedroom door, saying PRIVATE, KEEP OUT just for the night, while it was their room.

"Are you bringing pyjamas, or a nightie?" Rose asked Shireen.

"I only have nighties," said Shireen. "My best one is green with red sleeves. I'll bring that. It's all soft and warm. It cost thirty pounds. It's the best quality."

"I shall wear a nightie too, then," said Rose. "Do you have slippers?"

"Yes," said Shireen cautiously, wondering whether Rose would laugh at her slippers, which had panda faces on them, and ears.

"I have hippo slippers," said Rose. "Grey furry hippos with blue eyes."

So that was all right.

4 Preparations

Rose came home from school on her own as usual. The key was behind the big tub of flowers, where it had been hiding on Monday. Tanya was peeping over the fence.

"Want to come over and play?" she asked. "The baby's asleep, so you don't have to watch her being fed."

"No thanks," said Rose, picking out the key and dusting her hands off.

"Can I come over to yours, then?" said Tanya. "It's boring here when the baby's asleep."

"Sorry," said Rose. "My best friend Shireen's coming round. I have to get things ready for her."

"Is that the new girl in your class?" asked Tanya. "I thought I was your best friend."

"You'll always be my best neighbour," said Rose. "But I have to have friends as well, don't I?"

"Best neighbour isn't much," said Tanya. "I'm your only neighbour, except for our baby and that old man with the cat. So don't you want to play with me any more, then?"

"I expect I will sometimes," said Rose. "But I'm afraid this afternoon I have to get ready for my friend coming. She's going to stay the night. We're sleeping in my mother's bed."

"I hope your friend doesn't wet the bed, then," said Tanya.

"Of course she doesn't," said Rose. "We're having Chokky Pops for breakfast. My mum bought a big packet specially. And we're going to have a midnight feast. I'm only telling you because you're my best neighbour. You mustn't tell anyone else, or I'll kill you."

"Can I come round for the midnight feast?" asked Tanya. "I've never been to one."

"Sorry," said Rose. "I don't see how you could

get into our house in the middle of the night
without anyone hearing, do you? Besides, it's
really just for us two, because we're best friends.
I'll have to go now. Bye!"

Tanya watched over the fence as Rose
disappeared round the side of the house. It would
be years before the baby would be old enough to
have midnight feasts. And Tanya's mum never
bought Chokky Pops. They just had toast for
breakfast if they were lucky.

Rose checked the bedroom. The ironed sheet
and pillowcases looked very smooth. It was a pity
that Mum was not a proper mother who had a
dressing table with lots of make-up on it. That
would have been fun. Rose fetched her best
nightie and put it under one of the pillows. She
put her slippers neatly beside the bed.

Then she went downstairs and washed up the
breakfast things, and dried them and put them
away, so that the kitchen would look perfect for
Shireen. When Liz came in, Rose was polishing
the knives and forks and spoons with a clean tea-
towel to shine them up.

"I thought you were having beefburgers in buns

for tea?" said Liz. "You won't need knives and forks."

"Shireen is a very polite person," said Rose. "She may be used to eating everything with a knife and fork. And if she does, I will too."

"If she's a very polite person," said Liz, "I shouldn't think she'll be your best friend for very long. Not once she's seen the way you eat."

"I hope you're not going to be rude and nasty while my friend is here," said Rose.

"I hope your friend is not as rude and nasty as you always are," said Liz. She made herself a cup of tea and picked up her school bag. "I'm going to do my homework in my bedroom," she said. "Please don't disturb me."

"Your bedroom!" said Rose. "It's my bedroom too!"

"I thought you were having Mum's bedroom for tonight," said Liz. "You can't have two rooms, you know." She went out, banging her bag against the door.

As soon as Mum came in, Rose ran across to the front door.

"Hello," said Mum, but Rose ran straight past her. "Where are you off to?" said Mum.

"Just watching out for Shireen," said Rose. "She said she would be here at twenty to six."

"I expect she's on her way," said Mum. "I'll just get changed, and then I'll get the tea started."

At last Shireen came in sight at the end of the street, carrying one handle of her bag while her mother carried the other. When Shireen saw Rose, she dropped her handle and ran towards her.

"Hello!" she said. Then she whispered, "I've brought two pies, and some cheese, and some raisins, and a can of lemonade!"

"Good," said Rose. "Come upstairs, quick."

Rose showed Shireen the big bedroom. They looked at Mum's shoes, and they looked at the food that Rose had stored in her drawer. Now it was at the bottom of Mum's wardrobe. The banana didn't look very fresh.

"You don't wet the bed, do you?" said Rose.

"Of course not," said Shireen.

"It's just that my next-door neighbour sometimes does," said Rose. "But of course she's younger than us. I suppose she couldn't come and have the feast with us, could she?"

"It wouldn't really be possible, would it?" said Shireen. "Anyway, it'll be more fun with just the two of us."

Rose showed Shireen all her teddies. It would have been all right for Shireen to bring her poodle after all. Rose showed her the space station she had made out of Lego.

"Oh," said Shireen. "Do you still play with Lego?"

They heard the parents talking downstairs. Then Shireen's mother called out, "Goodbye." Shireen hardly noticed her leaving.

"Where's your sister?" Shireen asked. She was not looking forward to meeting Liz. She imagined her very large and dangerous.

"She's doing her homework in my bedroom," said Rose. "We'll see her at tea-time. I hope she's not in a bad mood."

At tea-time Liz came silently into the kitchen and sat down. She was not quite as big as Shireen had expected, but Shireen thought she looked very fierce. They ate their beefburgers with their fingers and got lemonade bubbles up their noses. Liz drank tea like a grown-up, although Rose was sure she would really rather have had lemonade.

After tea, they played. They wanted to play 'Race to the Enchanted Castle', but the box was in Rose's bedroom and Rose said that Liz would kill her if she went in to fetch it.

"You go," Rose said. "Knock on the door and say, 'Please may I fetch a game.' She can't refuse a visitor."

But Shireen didn't dare, so they played battleships instead, and boxes, and telegraph-messages. Then they had a shower, and made the bathroom very wet, and brushed their teeth, and didn't get them very clean.

"Goodnight," said Mum. "Sleep well, Shireen. I'll leave the hall light on in case you wake in the night. Just call me if there's anything you want."

"We won't wake in the night, will we, Shireen?" said Rose. "We're tired. I think we shall go straight to sleep."

"Oh, yes," said Shireen, pretending to yawn. "I'm very tired. Goodnight."

Mum turned out the light and closed the door and Rose and Shireen giggled.

"Only four hours to go," whispered Rose. "Who's going to tell the first story?"

"You can," Shireen whispered back. "But no headless ghosts and no scary noises. And no dripping blood. It's a shame, but the doctor said it would be really bad for me to have any more nightmares."

After the first few stories, Rose began to yawn.

"Don't fall asleep," said Shireen. "It's only ten to nine."

"I won't fall asleep," said Rose, but her eyelids were heavy.

When Rose's mum's alarm clock said nine o'clock, Rose fell over on the bed, and when Shireen shook her, she didn't open her eyes. She just snorted quietly.

"Wake up!" Shireen whispered. But Rose was fast asleep.

Shireen didn't feel sleepy at all. She didn't think she ever would feel sleepy in this strange room. It was much bigger than her room at home, and the ceiling seemed a long way off. There were funny shadows in the corners.

I'll get into bed, she thought. Then I won't feel so cold. She squeezed in under the big quilt and pulled it up round her ears. I wish I had Poodle

here, she thought. She reached out for one of Rose's teddies, and tucked it in beside her. It felt nice and woolly, but it didn't smell right. Still, it was better than nothing.

Supposing I kick Rose by mistake, in my sleep? she thought. She had never shared a bed with someone else before. She might think that I did it on purpose and not be my friend any more.

Suddenly, Shireen remembered Rose asking whether she ever wet the bed. Of course she hardly ever did, but it would be so embarrassing, especially in Rose's mother's bed. She would die of shame.

"I won't go to sleep," she said to herself. "Then I can't wet the bed."

But as soon as she had decided not to go to sleep, she felt her eyes beginning to close. She sat up suddenly. That's no good, she thought. One of us has to stay awake until midnight, or we'll miss our feast.

But even sitting up, she could hardly keep her head upright. It kept falling to one side with a jerk.

Then she remembered the little alarm clock on the window-sill. I can put it under my pillow, thought Shireen. It'll wake me, and then I can wake Rose, and we can have our feast.

She climbed over Rose, who grunted, and picked up the clock. She was not sure how it worked. There were several knobs and keys on the back. One of the knobs had a picture of a bell next to it. Shireen turned it, and the little silver alarm hand moved round. Shireen set it at twelve. She wound the clock, and hoped that it would work. She tucked it under her pillow.

Then she fell asleep.

5   Midnight

BRRRRRRRRRRRRRRRRR!!!!!!!!!!

Shireen woke with a terrible jump and knew at once what she must do. She must find the clock and stop it ringing. But it seemed to have moved while she was asleep, and the noise went on and on while she felt under the pillow and then flung the pillow on the floor, and finally found the clock, pressed the knob on the top, and stopped the ringing. The noise carried on in her ears, rattling inside her head.

She lay quite still for a minute, wide awake. She had never guessed that the little clock would make such a loud noise. Rose's mum must have heard it. In a moment she would come in and be angry. Shireen quickly put the clock back on the window-sill, picked up her pillow, and closed her eyes. She would pretend to be asleep when Rose's mum came in, and perhaps Rose's mum would not be quite certain that it was this room that the noise had come from.

Shireen listened. There was no sound from the rest of the house, except a buzzing noise, which might be the fridge. Rose was still sleeping soundly. Perhaps they were all sound sleepers in this family, and none of them had heard the noise. In a minute Shireen would wake Rose, and they could have their feast. Shireen opened her eyes and looked at the clock. Four minutes past twelve. One more minute, and it would be safe to say that Rose's mum had not woken up.

Suddenly, there was a click in the passage outside. It could have been a door shutting. Shireen closed her eyes and pulled the quilt up to her nose. Yes, there was a creak. Someone stepping on a loose floorboard. She couldn't hear footsteps, but then Rose's mum would be in bare feet, or wearing soft slippers. Shireen held her breath. She heard the bedroom door open.

Someone was coming in. Surely Rose's mum would see that they were both asleep, and tiptoe out again.

But no, the light was switched on. Shireen could see it red through her eyelids. Then she felt the quilt snatched off her face.

She tried to carry on pretending to sleep, but it was impossible, with her eyes screwed up tight against the glaring electric light. She looked up and saw Liz standing over her. The terrible Liz.

"What's going on?" said Liz. "Who set off the alarm clock?"

"I don't know," whispered Shireen. "I'm sorry it woke you up."

"Wake up, Rose," said Liz, stepping up on to the bed and walking over Shireen. She shook her sister hard, but Rose, even with no quilt over her, carried on sleeping.

"Useless," said Liz. "Sleeps like a pig." She gave Rose a last kick and sat down on the bed next to Shireen. "Why did you set the alarm, anyway?" she asked. "Midnight feast?"

Shireen just stared up at Liz, not daring even to nod or shake her head.

"Come on, then," said Liz. "Let's get started. Where's the food?"

"I don't know," whispered Shireen, still staring at Liz.

Liz looked round the room, wondering where the food might be hidden. She peered under the bed, behind the curtain, in Shireen's bag, and then in the wardrobe. She pulled out Rose's plastic bag and looked inside.

"Mouldy banana," she said. "The rest of the stuff looks all right. Hang on a minute, there's a cake downstairs. Shall I run down and get us a bit?"

Shireen shook her head. Rose's mum would be sure to hear if Liz started running round the house and things would be even worse. But Liz was already at the door.

"Lay it all out on the bed," she said, "ready for when I get back."

As soon as Liz had closed the door, Shireen turned round and shook Rose. "Rose, you've got to wake up! It's twelve o'clock, and Liz is going to eat all our food! Rose!"

Shaking was no use. She whispered as loudly as she dared into Rose's ear. Eventually she pulled Rose's hair.

"Wer?" mumbled Rose. "Worra morra morra hair?"

"Liz is going to eat our midnight feast!" said Shireen. "Wake up!"

"All right," said Rose. "In a minute." Then

she was fast asleep again.

Liz came back with a chunk of cherry cake.
"Come on," she said. "Let's get started. Do you
want some cake?"

Shireen just looked at Liz.

"It's midnight," said Liz. "You want a
midnight feast, don't you?"

"But what about Rose?" said Shireen. "It's her
feast, too."

"Well," said Liz, "if she won't wake up, there's
nothing we can do about it. She wouldn't want it
to be wasted, would she?"

Shireen didn't dare disagree with Liz. She took
a piece of cherry cake and ate it. It was delicious.

Liz took the lemonade can and opened it with a
pop. Shireen listened nervously for Rose's mum,
but the rest of the house was quiet. They had a
drink each, and Liz shared out the sweets.

"Save some for Rose," said Shireen. "They
were her sweets. She can have them in the
morning."

"You can save some of your share if you want,"
said Liz. "And she can have the banana. Shall I
tell you what happened when I had a midnight

feast at my friend Victoria's house?"

Shireen nodded. Her mouth was full.

"Victoria has this big old house, with a huge attic that no-one ever goes in. We went up into the attic at midnight. It was pitch black, and cobwebs kept brushing against our faces, and we could hear the church clock striking twelve. There was a big water-tank in the attic, and all the time it was making a sort of sucking noise, and a *drip-drip-drip*, and Victoria said it sounded like blood dripping."

"What did you have for your midnight feast?" Shireen asked quickly.

"Carrots, spring onions, lettuce, cucumber, apples, pears, grapes," said Liz. "Victoria's father works at the greengrocer's. Anyway, we were

sitting there eating, when there was a sort of swishing noise behind us, and when we looked round, there was a big dark shape. It looked like a woman dressed in a long gown, but where her head should have been, there wasn't anything. She was holding her head under her arm, and her eyes were staring ..."

"Something like that happened to me once," said Shireen hurriedly. She thought she would rather talk about ghosts than hear about them. "It

was on holiday. I was staying with my great-aunt. She lives in a castle in a dark pine wood."
Shireen found that she was rather good at making up scary stories. Liz thought so too.

"It's good fun having a midnight feast with you," Liz said. "Rose gets scared if you talk about ghosts, but you don't."

Shireen felt very proud.

"Shall we play 'Race to the Enchanted Castle'?"
Liz suggested. "It's a really good game, all about
witches and ghosts. I'll get it from my bedroom.
Mum won't wake up. She sleeps like a log, just
like Rose."

After the game, they told each other jokes.
Then at two o'clock Liz said it was time to go to
sleep. She took the game back to her room, and
Shireen swept the crumbs out of the bed and fell
asleep.

6 Chokky Pops

When Rose woke up it was already light. What
had happened? Had Shireen turned the light on?
But Shireen was fast asleep, and the light was
coming in through the curtains. Rose reached up
for the alarm clock which Mum kept on her
window-sill. It was not quite in its usual place. It
said half-past seven.

Half-past seven! Midnight had gone by, and
they had not had their feast. They must have
fallen asleep. Rose remembered sitting up with
Shireen, telling stories. She remembered feeling
sleepy. How stupid of them. They should have
told their stories standing up, then they wouldn't
have fallen asleep.

Poor Shireen would be so disappointed. Never mind. Rose would get the food out, and wake Shireen, and they could have an early-morning feast instead. Mum and Liz never got up before nine on a Saturday morning, so they would have plenty of time. It would be nearly as good as a midnight feast.

Rose climbed carefully over Shireen and tiptoed to the wardrobe. She lifted out the plastic bag. It felt very light. Something was wrong. Rose looked inside. The banana was still there, but all the packets looked crumpled and empty. She took out the lemonade can. It was open, and empty. There was half a chocolate biscuit and part of an apple and blackberry pie. There were a few sweets left in their packet, and a bit of cheese, looking dried-up and nasty.

It couldn't have been mice. Mice couldn't open a can of lemonade. Could it have been Liz? Could

Liz have guessed about the feast, and sneaked into their room, and eaten the food while they were asleep? Rose was about to wake Shireen, when she saw her friend's face. There was a smear on her cheek. It looked like chocolate. Rose looked round and saw a raisin on the pillow, and crumbs on the carpet by the bed.

"I thought you were my best friend!" Rose said through clenched teeth. "I'm never going to be your friend again!"

Shireen didn't wake up. Rose looked at her, and imagined her sitting up in bed at midnight, silently eating all the food by herself. "So you thought it would be nice if it was just the two of us, did you!" hissed Rose.

Shireen still didn't wake up. Rose thought she looked a little bit fatter since last night. It was not surprising.

"I've got a real friend, and I don't need you, greedy selfish Shireen!"

Rose took her clothes and got dressed in the bathroom. Then she went out to the yard because the house was not big enough to hold her enormous anger.

"Hello," said Tanya. "Where's your best friend? Did you have a good midnight feast?"

"Hello," said Rose. "She's not my best friend, and I never had a midnight feast."

"The baby was sick in my bed this morning," said Tanya. "Mum says I shouldn't have let her have two bottles of milk all at once, but I wasn't to know, was I?"

Rose kicked the fence.

"Have you had breakfast yet?" asked Tanya. "Those Chokky Pops?"

"No," said Rose.

"Aren't you hungry?" said Tanya. "I'm starving."

"Wait a moment," said Rose. She ran indoors and fetched the packet of Chokky Pops. Then she ran round the front of Tanya's house and down the alley to Tanya's back yard.

"Can I eat my breakfast at your house?" said Rose.

Tanya's mother had cleaned up the baby, and the baby was allowed to try some Chokky Pops too. She ate them with her fingers off the tray of her high chair, but Tanya and Rose had two huge bowls each, with milk, and nearly finished the packet.

"That was a feast," said Tanya. They were both full up. "I'd rather have a feast for breakfast. In the middle of the night I would be too tired to taste it properly."

They read all of the packet and washed up their bowls.

"I've learnt a new kind of hopscotch," said Tanya. "My cousins taught it to me. Do you want to try it?"

They went out into the yard. The sun was just coming over the roofs now, so Tanya's mum put the baby out in her high chair to watch them playing.

"She won't be sick again, will she?" said Rose.

"No," said Tanya. "Those Chokky Pops will have done her the world of good."

"You can be my best friend if you want," said Rose.

"You can be mine if you want," said Tanya.

Just then Shireen looked through the broken place in the fence. "Rose," she said.

Rose carried on hopping, and only stopped when she had zigzagged all the way up and down the new sort of hopscotch.

"What is it?" she said coldly.

"Your mum told me to call you in for breakfast," said Shireen.

Rose was surprised, Mum didn't usually get up this early on a Saturday. It must be because of having a visitor in the house.

"All right," she said. "I'm coming. I'll get the cereal. There isn't much left."

"That's all right," said Shireen. "I'm not very hungry. Rose, I'm sorry about the midnight feast. Liz said we had to have it, because it was midnight. I tried to wake you up, but you just wouldn't. And I did save some for you."

"Saved some for me!" said Rose. "Only a rotten banana and some of my own sweets!"

She went into Tanya's kitchen to fetch the Chokky Pops packet. Tanya had had her turn of hopping. She thought about what Rose had said. "A banana?" she said. "My baby loves bananas. Can I mash it up for her?"

Rose came out into the yard again.

"I did save half an apple and blackberry pie for you," said Shireen.

Rose didn't answer her.

"I'll see you later, Tan," she said. "We'll have another game of hopscotch."

She came round into her own yard and Shireen followed her silently into the kitchen. Mum was watching some toast under the grill. Her hair was sticking up in tufts. She hadn't brushed it yet. Rose put the Chokky Pops packet on the table and sat down. Shireen sat shyly at the other end.

"Cereal, Shireen?" Mum asked. "Rose said you like those chocolate things."

"No, thank you," said Shireen.

Mum turned round with two more slices of bread in her hand. "No Chokky Pops? Rose, you told me they were Shireen's favourite!" She meant that she wouldn't have bought them just as a treat for Rose.

"Oh, they *are* my favourite," said Shireen. "I think I will have some after all."

She poured herself a very small bowl of cereal. Rose saw her take a big gulping swallow before she put the first spoonful in her mouth. Good, she was feeling too full after all that food in the night.

"Just watch this toast for me, will you, Rose, while I run up and do my hair," said Mum. "I wasn't sure whether anyone was still asleep in my room when I got up, so I didn't like to go in and get my things."

Rose looked at Shireen when Mum was out of the room. "I hope you tidied up," she said. "Or you'll be in for it."

Mum was not likely to miss the crumbs or crisps on the floor. She would probably notice other things that Rose had not spotted. She was an expert at noticing dirt.

Shireen chewed miserably at her Chokky Pops. Rose turned the toast over.

"Rose!" There was a shout from upstairs. Mum came thundering down the stairs, but when she came into the kitchen she spoke quietly, because of having a visitor there. "Rose, you know I said you were not to have any food in my bedroom. You've left it in a terrible mess. Don't worry, Shireen, I'm not angry with you. But Rose knew quite well."

Although Mum was not shouting, it was easy to see that she was angry. Rose was angry too. She clenched her teeth. It was bad enough to miss out on the feast, without being blamed for it as well.

"It wasn't Rose," said Shireen in a small voice. "Rose didn't eat anything. It was me."

"Well, it's very nice of you to say so," said Mum. She didn't sound as though she believed her. "Anyway, don't worry about it. Rose can clear up the mess later on." She sighed. "What am I going to do with you, Rose? It's not just the mess. I don't suppose Shireen's mother would have let her come to stay if she had known that she was going to be up half the night."

Rose remembered what Shireen had said out in the yard. 'Liz said we had to have the feast.' She had started to feel sorry for Shireen. The next time Shireen looked at her with pleading, apologetic eyes, Rose nodded, to show that she guessed that everything was Liz's fault.

"Let's forget about it," said Mum. "But I don't think it's a very nice way to treat your guest, Rose, to let her take the blame. You'd better make sure she has a really nice time from now on. What are you planning to do after breakfast? Liz says she feels sick so she's staying in bed."

Rose thought that if Liz was feeling ill that proved that she had been eating in the night. Rose tried to imagine what had happened. She did almost remember someone pulling her hair while she was asleep. At least Shireen had not selfishly eaten all the food on her own. That would have been too mean and greedy to forgive. Liz had made her eat it. Rose knew how Liz could make you do things. And Shireen had tried to protect Rose from Mum's anger.

Rose looked across at Shireen again. Shireen was still watching her anxiously. Rose smiled and the worried wrinkles in Shireen's forehead disappeared.

"Well," said Mum, moving Shireen's bowl away from her. "No wonder you don't want these Chokky Pops. Go on, you terrible girls. You'd better both go out and run around a bit and shake down all that food."

Rose and Shireen got up and went out to the yard.

"Thanks for trying to explain," said Rose. "But it doesn't matter. I'm used to Liz getting away with things. I don't suppose you'll want to come and stay again after all that fuss."

"My mum would have been much crosser than that," said Shireen. "I should have thought about clearing up the crumbs. Anyway, Liz didn't exactly get away with it if she feels ill."

"Maybe we won't bother with a midnight feast again," said Rose. "We'll think of something different."

"Anyway, it's your turn to come and stay at my house next time," said Shireen.

"Coming to play hopscotch?" Tanya shouted through the fence. "Or we could do skipping now that we've got three people. Do you know what?

My baby's just been sick again. It was all those Chokky Pops. She hadn't chewed them up at all."

Rose and Shireen ran round to Tanya's side of the fence. Tanya had tied one end of her skipping rope to the washing-pole.

"Shall we play 'I am a girl guide dressed in blue'?" said Rose. "I don't mind turning first." She took the loose end of the rope and began to chant:

> "I am a girl guide dressed in blue,
> These are the things that I must do,
> Bow to the King, salute to the Queen,
> And show my knickers to the Royal Marine."

While she watched Tanya and Shireen jump in and do the actions as they skipped over the turning rope, she wondered which of them was really her best friend.

Tanya trod on the rope. She untangled her
ankle and took the end from Rose.

"Your turn," she said breathlessly.

Rose jumped in next to Shireen. It was good
that the rope was long enough for two people to
skip together. It was good to have two best
friends.